Let's Clean Up!

Peggy Perry Anderson

sandpiper

Green Light Readers
HOUGHTON MIFFLIN HARCOURT
BOSTON NEW YORK

To my dear sister Linda,
whose housecleaning habits
forced me to ask for my own room.

Mother said,
"I have the broom.
Let's clean up
this messy room."

Mother cleaned high.

Mother cleaned low.

Mother cleaned the room for Joe.

"I have room to ride my train."

"I have room to fly my planes."

"I can race my racing cars."

"And launch my rocket to the stars."

"There's room to bounce upon my bed."

"Or room to hide below instead."

"I can build a tent today."

"Wait! THIS is the game
I have wanted to play!"

"What will I find inside the toy box?"

"Oh boy! Here are all of my building blocks!"

"I'll build a tower to the sky!"

It was then
that Mother
began to cry.

"Don't worry, Mom. I have the broom."

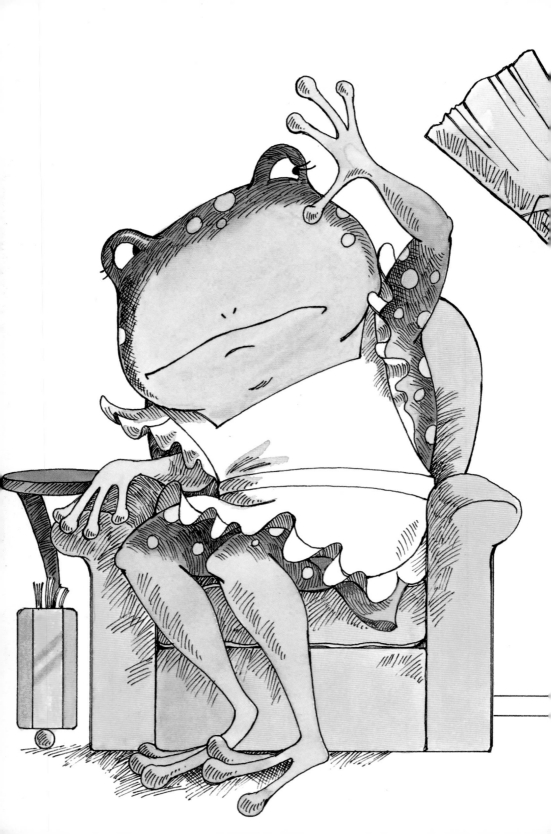

"I'll clean up this messy room!"

"My," said Mother, "you cleaned in a hurry."

"I told you, Mother, not to worry!"

"Oh, Mother, look and see."

"My room is as
clean as it can be."

"Oh, Joe, you worked so hard."

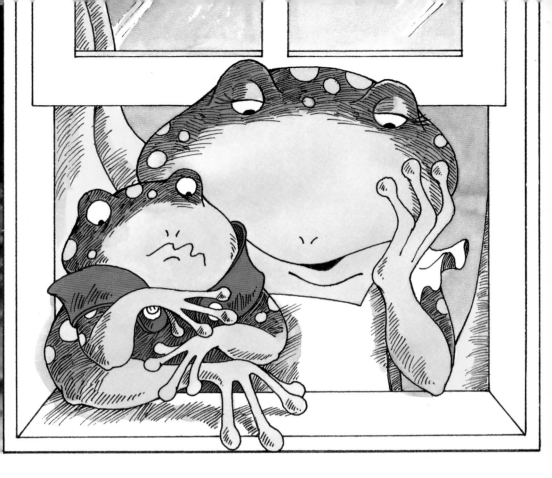

"Now what shall we do about the yard?"

Joe said,
"Mom you're right.
It's true.
To really clean
UP it takes
two!"